...THS
—THREE HEROIC TALES—

FOR TOM AND JULIE — H. L.

FOR MARION — D. M.

FOR MY BEAUTIFUL NOAH — C. H.

• • • • • • • • • • • • • • • • • • • • • • • • •

BIBLIOGRAPHY

Calasso, Roberto. *The Marriage of Cadmus and Harmony*. New York: Vintage, 1994.

Garfield, Leon and Edward Blishen. *The God Beneath the Sea*. Illustrated by Charles Keeping. London: Corgi, 1973.

Graves, Robert. *The Greek Myths*. London: Pelican Books, 1955.

——. *The White Goddess: A Historical Grammar of Poetic Myth*. London: Faber & Faber, 1948.

The Homeric Hymns. Translated by Jules Cashford. London: Penguin, 2003.

Kerényi, Carl. *Eleusis: Archetypal Image of Mother and Daughter*. Bollingen Series. Princeton, NJ: Princeton University Press, 1967.

March, Jenny. *Cassell's Dictionary of Classical Mythology*. London: Cassell Reference, 1998.

Ovid. *Metamorphoses*. Translated by Mary Innes. London: Penguin, 1955.

Schwab, Gustav. *Gods and Heroes*. New York: Pantheon, 1974.

• • • • • • • • • • • • • • • • • • • • • • • • •

Barefoot Books
2067 Massachusetts Ave
Cambridge, MA 02140

Barefoot Books
29 / 30 Fitzroy Square
London, W1T 6LQ

Text copyright © 2013 by Hugh Lupton
and Daniel Morden
Illustrations copyright © 2013 by Carole Hénaff
The moral rights of Hugh Lupton, Daniel Morden
and Carole Hénaff have been asserted

First published in three volumes (*Demeter and
Persephone*, *Theseus and the Minotaur* and *Orpheus
and Eurydice*) in the United States of America
by Barefoot Books, Inc and in Great Britain by
Barefoot Books, Ltd in 2013
This combined volume first published in 2017
All rights reserved

Graphic design by Ryan Scheife,
Mayfly Design, Minneapolis, MN
and Sarah Soldano, Barefoot Books
Edited and art directed by Kate DePalma
and Tessa Strickland, Barefoot Books
Reproduction by B & P International,
Hong Kong
Printed in China on 100% acid-free paper
This book was typeset in Agamemnon,
Dante MT Std, ITC Galliard and Mynaruse
The illustrations were prepared in acrylics

ISBN 978-1-78285-349-7

Library of Congress Cataloging-in-Publication
Data is available upon request

British Cataloguing-in-Publication Data:
a catalogue record for this book is available
from the British Library

1 3 5 7 9 8 6 4 2

GREEK MYTHS
—THREE HEROIC TALES—

RETOLD BY HUGH LUPTON & DANIEL MORDEN
ILLUSTRATED BY CAROLE HÉNAFF

Barefoot Books
step inside a story

CONTENTS

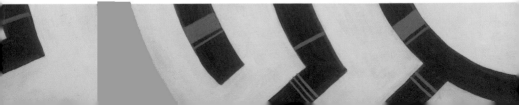

Glossary

Corona Borealis
(coh-ROH-nah boh-ree-AL-iss): a crown-shaped constellation

labyrinth *(LAH-beh-rinth):* a maze

lyre *(LIE-er):* a U-shaped stringed musical instrument

nymph *(NIMF):* a mythological nature spirit; usually a young woman

pomegranate *(POM-eh-gran-et):* a many-seeded fruit

pyre *(PIE-er):* a pile of wood for burning a body at a funeral

tyrant *(TIE-rant):* a cruel ruler

Place names

Athens *(AH-thens)*

Crete *(KREET)*

Eleusis *(el-EE-yoo-sis)*

Lesbos *(LEZ-boss)*

Mount Olympus
(MOUNT oh-LIM-pus)

Naxos *(NACKS-oss)*

Can you find each place on the map on page 136?

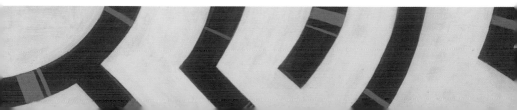

CHARACTERS IN THE STORY

DEMETER
(Dem-EET-er)
goddess of the harvest

PERSEPHONE
(per-SEH-fon-ee)
Demeter's daughter

ZEUS
(ZOOSE)
god of thunder

HADES
(HAY-deez)
god of the Underworld

THE NYMPH
(NIMF)
Demeter's friend

HERMES
(HER-meez)
messenger god

THE OLD WOMAN

THE OLD WOMAN'S DAUGHTER

DEMETER
···· AND ····
PERSEPHONE

INTO THIN AIR

IMAGINE THREE WORLDS. ONE world is above us. It is perfect, impossible, inhabited by bright immortals. Imagine Mount Olympus. On his throne sits sky god Zeus. He is all-powerful.

He is watching our world below.

Imagine another world, a world under ours. A world without hope or joy.

Mist. Silence. Bitter cold. The Land of the Dead. On his throne sits the lord of darkness, Hades, his eyes as dark and deep as open graves.

He is watching our world above.

In between these two worlds, imagine our green Earth, bursting with life, burgeoning growth. The air is heavy with the scent of flowers and the songs of birds. This world is ruled over by Demeter, goddess of the harvest.

Zeus above, Hades below, were watching. They were watching a female figure walking through a meadow.

This was Persephone, the daughter of Demeter. Persephone, that sweet young shoot, shining with youth and life, was gathering flowers with a nymph. She saw a poppy. She loved poppies. She knelt to pick one —

The ground cracked. The earth and air shook. A gaping gash appeared. It belched bitter, acrid fog. Behind them they could hear a deafening thunder. They looked over their

shoulders and stumbled at the sight. Hades!
The grim king himself, in a chariot drawn
by four Night Mares, burst forth from the
Underworld! He cracked his whip. His horses

hurtled towards them. Persephone and the nymph lifted up their skirts to flee. But already the king of terrors was towering over them. Hades leaned over the side of his chariot and plucked Persephone from the earth.

She called her mother's name, but there was no answer. The nymph flung out her hands and grasped Persephone's dress. The dress tore, and then the chariot was gone. It had plunged into the darkness below. The gash in the earth closed to a scar. The nymph was alone.

As she plunged into the gloom, Persephone kept calling her mother's name. But no one came to her call. Demeter was far away.

The nymph was beside herself. She cast about helplessly. She sank to her knees. At her feet were the flowers that Persephone had picked moments before: soft crocuses, bright irises, hyacinth, rosebuds and lilies, dying in the dirt. She tried to gather them, but they tumbled from her trembling hands. She wept. So profound was her grief that she melted into sorrow. Every pore of her body wept tears, until all that was left of her was a torn dress floating in a salty pool.

Demeter, the goddess of growth, the bringer of life, of the crown of corn, of the lustrous hair, whom we must thank for every full mouth and every bulging belly. Demeter, far above on Mount Olympus, caught a snatch of sound. She was pierced with fear. She called her daughter's name: there came no reply. She descended to the earth. She searched the world. Neither Eos, goddess of the dawn, nor Hesperus, the evening star, found her resting. As she passed by, the flowers wilted. Anguish aged her. Her crown of corn fell from her brow.

Her lustrous hair turned dirty grey. Her radiant robes were ripped to rags.

For nine days, for nine nights, with a flaming torch in each hand, she searched the earth. The wind moaned. The sky cried. Once in the early morning a shepherd saw her searching, her face a mask of anguish, marked with shadow and fire. She was a pitiful sight. He turned away and uttered a prayer.

THE STRANGE GUEST

ONE DAY, BROKEN, SOBBING, Demeter sat by a well.

Nearby the well there was a cottage. In the cottage lived an old woman, her daughter and the daughter's child, a baby boy.

The grandmother saw this stranger sitting by the well. She saw the fine clothes ripped to rags. Beneath the filth the stranger was beautiful.

The grandmother drew water from the well with a bronze pitcher. She offered some to the stranger. The stranger sipped. She

scraped the tears from her cheeks with the
heel of her hand.

"Come out of the wind and the rain.
Come with me now," said the grandmother.
She took the stranger's hand in her own.
Silently, the stranger stood. She let herself be
led into the cottage.

The baby was crying. He'd been crying
all morning. The sight of the stranger silenced
him. He stretched out his scrawny arms.

"Look at that!" said the grandmother.
"Daughter, give him to her!"

The daughter looked dubiously at the filthy
visitor. The grandmother smiled and urged her,
"Go on!"

She handed the child to the stranger. The
baby smiled and cooed. He opened his little
hands. The grandmother laughed. "You have
the touch!"

That night the stranger stayed with them. She said little and ate nothing. But they could see the presence of the child brought her comfort. And the baby was happy, serene.

THE PROMISE

THE NEXT MORNING THE BABY looked for the stranger. The mother was exhausted, and there seemed no harm in this woman, so she passed him over. The stranger took the child gratefully. She cradled him. For a moment she looked up and smiled. The mother was taken aback. Never had she seen such a stare! Her eyes were golden, like the sun.

The mother said, "Have you any children?"

"I have a daughter," said the stranger.

"Is she married?" asked the mother.

Tears spattered onto the baby's face.

"She is gone."

The mother was suddenly filled with pity. "Why don't you stay with us? You could look after my son. We'd be glad of your help," she offered.

"I will tend to him at night. You sleep in the bedroom. I'll care for him here," said the stranger.

"A few nights' sleep would be a blessing!" the mother said.

The stranger said, "Then don't come through at night. Don't even look. Stay in there, no matter what you hear. Do you promise?"

That stare again . . .

"I promise."

"No harm will come to the child," the stranger promised.

The days turned to weeks; the weeks turned to months. The stranger stayed with them. Mostly she was silent, mute with grief.

The baby thrived. The mother and the grandmother were amazed. He had been a whining runt. Now he was chubby, healthy, happy. He was so beautiful...like a god.

One night, in her bedroom, the mother was woken by the sound of her son chuckling in the room beyond. Curious, she crept to the door. She opened it a crack.

The stranger was holding the baby by his ankle, dangling him in the flames of the fire. He wriggled and giggled, and as the flames tickled his arms, his back, his chest, the mother screamed.

"What are you doing?"

The stranger looked up. She lifted the baby from the fire and laid him carefully on the flagstones. She said, "If only you had kept your promise. I was burning away his mortality. He would never have died. He would have cheated

the three Fates. But now he'll grow old and wither, like the rest of you."

She strode into the dark.

Chapter Four

THE TRUTH COMES OUT

THE NEXT NIGHT, IN THE village of Eleusis, there was a feast. A strange woman came out of the darkness to watch the dancing and revelry. A cluster of farmworkers, drinking by the fire, noticed her and stared. She stared back. They looked away.

"Hey! Swineherd!" said one. "Tell that story again!"

"What story?" said the swineherd.

"Of who you saw," another one said.

The men laughed. The swineherd frowned and said, "How many times have I told you? It was Hades! It was! First there were two maidens gathering flowers. Pretty things they were; eyes like buds. Then this crack appeared in the ground. Hades came out in his chariot! He grabbed one of them and took her under!"

The men hooted with laughter. But in an instant the stranger had grabbed the swineherd's arm, her golden eyes fixed on him.

"Tell me where."

He told her all that he knew.

Demeter flew to the place. She found the scar in the earth and beside it a salty pool.

The nymph wanted to speak. She wanted to tell the terrible news about Persephone, but her lips, her tongue, her mouth were just water now. So with her shifting currents she summoned the torn dress.

Demeter knew it at once. She sank to her knees. The grass around her wilted and died. The trees wept their leaves. The corn in the fields withered and dried in the husk. The apples, the figs, rotted as they grew. The ground cracked and crumbled. Clouds of dust blotted out the eye of the sun. Everywhere there was want, hunger, suffering, famine, death. Desperate, men became no better than beasts. Children throttled their parents for a crust.

News spread. Demeter walked the earth, searching for her child. The people made temples and altars to her. They gave her whatever scant offerings they could find. They begged her to show them mercy, entreating her to give life back to the land. But she heard only the distant cry of her child, the cry that had first summoned her from the sky.

ZEUS STEPS IN

U P ON MOUNT OLYMPUS, Zeus shuddered. The earth was screaming. This was not in his plan. He sent the messenger of the gods, Hermes, to fetch Demeter. Hermes commanded her in the name of Zeus to accompany him. But it was as though she'd been turned to stone. The only signs of life were the tears carving grooves in her cheeks. Silver-tongued Hermes tried to persuade her. His words could charm the wings from the back of a bird, but not even he could move her.

Zeus sent every god and goddess to Demeter offering gifts, to beg, wheedle and cajole her.

Eventually Zeus had to descend from the heavens himself. For him, she turned her head: "You gave my child to the god of death. Since he has her for a wife, let him have the earth for a dowry. This world will be his. Let it be as dark and desolate as his realm."

"Your daughter is a queen," Zeus said. "She sits beside the king of shadows. You should be proud of her."

"Persephone does not belong below. She loves the warmth of the sun on her skin. She loves birdsong. Down there she hears only the moans of the dead," said Demeter.

Zeus looked about. He heard no prayers in his name, only screams and suffering. The only burnt offering that rose into the sky was the smoke of funeral pyres.

"You know the laws. There are forces to which even I must answer. The three Fates have decreed: Persephone will be freed...provided she has not tasted Hades's food."

THE COMPROMISE

S O HERMES DESCENDED TO the Land of the Dead. As he crossed the plain he saw poppies growing, each like a shimmering drop of blood. He followed their trail to the hall of the grim king.

"Mighty Zeus has decreed: Persephone must be freed, unless she has tasted your food," said wing-heeled Hermes.

Something flickered in the caves of Hades's eyes. He bowed his head.

"Very well."

Persephone returned to the earth. When Demeter saw her daughter, her heart opened like a flower. The soil grew long ears of corn like waving hair, the whole wide earth was fragrant with blooms and blossom. She stretched out her hands. Persephone reached for her mother, but Demeter saw on her daughter's palm a stain as red as blood.

"What is that mark?" she asked Persephone.

"Only the juice of a pomegranate."

"Did you eat?"

Persephone looked at her mother. "Six seeds," she said.

In the darkness below, the king of terrors grinned.

Demeter returned to Zeus.

"I have been tricked again! Imagine a world where nothing green grows, a world without hope or joy, where no birds sing, where night blots out the eye of day. This is not the Land of the Dead that I describe," said Demeter. "This will be the Land of the Living, unless you give me back my daughter."

Zeus found a compromise.

Ever since then, for six months of the year — six months for six seeds — Persephone lives with Hades in the Land of the Dead. The moment she departs, her mother Demeter's heart turns cold with grief, so our world is silent, dark and desolate.

And for six months Persephone lives here on the earth with her mother. The moment she returns, Demeter is filled with joy, and from the earth comes new life, budding, burgeoning growth. There is light, warmth, birdsong.

After Zeus's judgement, Demeter returned to the people of Eleusis, the people who had looked after her in her anguish. She taught

them the rituals they must observe to welcome Persephone back to the world, rituals that would ensure that their harvests would always be plentiful.

So it was and so it is.

MORE ABOUT THE MYTH

Where do Greek myths come from? There is not one single book or source that records them all. The myths come from different poems, plays, stories and other writings from both Greek and Roman authors. The most detailed version of the myth of Demeter and Persephone comes to us from an ancient Greek poem called "To Demeter." Historians aren't sure who wrote it.

The story of Demeter and Persephone has inspired many famous works of art, including Italian artist Gian Lorenzo Bernini's breathtaking sculpture of Hades carrying Persephone away (created 1621–1622) and Russian composer Igor Stravinsky's musical piece *Perséphone* (first performed in 1934).

DEMETER is one of the Twelve Olympians, making her one of the most important Greek deities. She is the goddess of agriculture and the harvest, and is often shown in ancient artwork with a bundle (or "sheaf") of wheat.

PERSEPHONE, whose father is Zeus, is also known by the name Kore, which means "maiden." She appears in the myth of Orpheus and Eurydice as Hades's wife and the Queen of the Underworld.

Demeter and Persephone were worshipped throughout ancient Greece every autumn at the Thesmophoria festival, which marked the time of the year when Persephone entered the Underworld.

CHARACTERS IN THE STORY

THESEUS
(THEE-see-us)
son of King Aegus

THE MINOTAUR
(MY-noh-tor)
the monster of Minos;
also named Asterius

KING MINOS
(MY-noss)
King of Crete

KING AEGEUS
(ee-GEE-us)
King of Athens

ATHENE
(ah-THEE-nee)
goddess of wisdom

DAEDALUS
(DYE-dull-us)
an inventor

TALOS
(TAH-loss)
Daedalus's nephew

PASIPHAE
(pah-SIFF-aye)
Queen of Crete

ARIADNE
(ah-REE-ad-nee)
Minos and Pasiphae's
daughter

ICARUS
(ICK-ar-us)
Daedalus's son

AEGLE
(AYE-glay)
Theseus's girlfriend

DIONYSUS
(DYE-oh-nice-us)
god of wine

THESEUS
AND THE
MINOTAUR

THE JEALOUS UNCLE

I MAGINE A TYRANT. IMAGINE a king so powerful, so fearsome, that other kings from all over the world sent him ships laden with treasures and tributes each month to appease him. Minos of Crete was such a king.

One of the kings who sent him treasure was the ruler of a city far away to the north, King Aegeus of Athens.

Owl-eyed Athene, the goddess of war and wisdom, loved the city of Athens. She loved the people of Athens. Most of all she loved people who were like her — quick and clever, crafty and cunning.

She was particularly fond of an inventor called Daedalus. He had made a sword so sharp that it never struck in battle without killing its victim. He had made a room in the root of a volcano that was warm in the coldest of winters. He had made a honeycomb out of gold that was so lifelike that bees would crawl across it searching for sweetness.

But the one Athene loved most was Daedalus's nephew, Talos. He was the cleverest of them all. When he was eight he had invented the first maze, a labyrinth for his pet rat. When he was ten he had invented the first kite, made from the feathers of a bird. Now he was twelve, and he was sitting with his uncle eating fish stew in their home high above the sea. When the stew was finished he reached into his bowl and pulled out a fish's jawbone. He felt the row of sharp teeth with the tip of his finger. Suddenly he smiled to himself and dropped the bone.

Daedalus watched the boy. He wondered what was running through his mind.

The next morning Daedalus woke up to hear a strange rasping sound. Talos had fashioned the very first saw, with a row of bronze teeth like the teeth of a fish. He was cutting through a piece of wood.

Daedalus was filled with jealous rage — a bitter, yellow, bubbling, seething rage that he couldn't control. Why hadn't he thought of that himself? Mad with jealousy, he grabbed the boy by the scruff of the neck and hurled him over the edge of the cliff. Talos fell, flailing, plunging, tumbling through the air.

But nothing is hidden from the eyes of the mighty gods and goddesses. Athene saw her

beloved boy falling and came to his rescue. All
at once, Talos felt feathers, black and white
feathers, pushing out of his arms. He felt
feathers pushing out of his body. He felt his

lips hardening into a beak. He felt a plume of feathers bursting out of the top of his head. The goddess had turned him into a bird, a lapwing, the very first of its kind. Talos beat his feathered arms against the air and flew, a strange lifting, tumbling flight, never very far from the ground. For the lapwing is the only bird afraid of heights — Talos has never forgotten his terrible fall.

THE INVENTOR'S CHALLENGE

WHEN KING AEGEUS HEARD that Daedalus had tried to murder his nephew, he sent soldiers to seize him so that he could be punished for his crime. But Daedalus was too quick for them and made his escape. He climbed onto a boat that was sailing south to Crete.

King Minos and his queen, Pasiphae, welcomed the famous inventor. Daedalus brought them gifts. To Minos he gave a bronze

map of his island kingdom: every hill, every river was etched into the shining surface. To Queen Pasiphae he gave a jointed statue, the perfect likeness of a human being, which could be moved into any posture. To their daughter, Princess Ariadne, he gave a golden crown. It was made of pure gold, and with a single spark from striking one stone against another, it could be set aflame, filling even the darkest of nights with brightness. Very quickly Daedalus earned the trust and admiration of the king.

One night he was summoned to the king's private chambers.

"It must seem to you that I want for nothing," said Minos. "I am rich. I have a fleet of ships that strikes terror into the hearts of countless kings. But the gods are cruel! The one thing they deny me is a son. What is the point of an empire without an heir? You above all other mortals are a maker of solutions. Make me a solution. Make me a son, and in return I will make you rich!"

Daedalus bowed his head and set to work. He made a solution: a potion that Queen Pasiphae had to drink on a special night when the moon was in the constellation of the bull. Queen Pasiphae became pregnant. Minos was overjoyed. He showered gifts on Daedalus.

"It is a son! I know it is a son. What name shall we give him?" the king asked Pasiphae.

"It is thanks to the stars that he came to us. We should thank the stars for him," she replied.

So they agreed the child would be called Asterius, which means "of the stars."

A CHILD IS BORN

THE DAYS TURNED TO WEEKS. The weeks turned to months. After five months, Pasiphae was huge with child. Six, seven, eight months — she could no longer walk. She took to her bed. After another month when the baby was due, Minos was fetched. He sent away the midwives. He wanted to be the first to lay eyes on his son... But when the baby appeared, the king looked on in horror. The child had the head and the horns of a bull!

"Fetch Daedalus!" cried Minos.

A servant brought Daedalus from his quarters. Minos pointed at his son with a trembling hand. "Look at it! Look what you've done! Get rid of it!"

"No!" exclaimed Pasiphae. "You will not kill my child!"

Daedalus looked from raving king to sobbing queen. Somehow he had to please them both.

"Great king, I have a solution. I'll make a prison for him — a secure place from which he will never escape."

In the caves beneath the palace, Daedalus set to work. Remembering the maze his nephew Talos had made for his pet rat, he constructed a labyrinth. It was a labyrinth of such complexity that if any human being — apart from its maker — took three steps into it they would become utterly lost. In the middle of the maze he hollowed out a chamber. A chute was dug from the palace above, down which food and drink could be lowered.

One night, while horn-headed Asterius was fast asleep, Daedalus took him in his arms and carried him into the maze. He placed him in the central chamber and slipped away.

Up above, Queen Pasiphae stood at the top of the chute. She heard her son wake, and cry for his mother — he cried and cried, while she stood helpless in the room above. But he did not die. He ate the food and drink that were lowered down to him. Down in the dark maze beneath the palace, Asterius was growing bigger and stronger by the day.

·········· Chapter Four ··········

A Monster is Born

THE DAYS TURNED TO WEEKS.
The weeks turned to months. The
months turned to years. Fifteen years went by.
Queen Pasiphae went to her husband.

"It is so long since we heard anything from…
below," she said. "I'm afraid he may be dead."

Minos sent a human chain into the labyrinth,
a chain of servants holding hands so that they
would not get lost in the twisting tunnels of the
maze. The king and queen stood at the top of the
chute. They heard sniffing… shouts of alarm…

bellowing…shouting…ripping…screaming…
tearing…chewing…and then silence.

Daedalus crept into the maze to see what
had happened. When he returned he reported
to Minos, "He ate them, your highness. Why
shouldn't he? He has been given the flesh of

cows to eat. No one has told him it is wrong to eat the flesh of men and women."

From then on Asterius refused all other food. He threw himself against the walls of his prison. He snorted and roared. There was no peace in the palace. Not even Minos could listen to the sound of his hungry son, bellowing for food and dying for lack of it. So he sent seven young men into the maze. Then another seven. Only young men were sent in, for Minos hated the sight of them. Whenever he saw one he was reminded of his own son, that thing of shame skulking in the shadows.

Daedalus shuddered. He had a secret son, whose mother was a Cretan slave girl. He was a beautiful, golden-haired boy called Icarus. Daedalus knew that if Minos learned of the boy's existence he would be filled with jealousy and send him to a horrible death. So he kept Icarus hidden in a secret chamber in his private quarters.

But soon there were no longer enough young men left on Crete to feed the monster. So Daedalus went to Minos and said, "The surrounding kingdoms all fear you. What if you were to demand that each kingdom send seven young men a year in tribute? Asterius would never want for food again."

CHAPTER FIVE

THE KING'S SACRIFICE

AND SO THE DECREE WENT out. Each kingdom sent seven young men: seven young men who would never be heard of again. Stories crossed from Crete with trading ships, stories of a flesh-eating beast beneath Minos's palace called the Minotaur.

Soon it was Athens's turn. But King Aegeus resisted, unable to bring himself to send seven young Athenians to a horrible death. Furious, Minos ordered a fleet of ships to sail to Athens with himself in command.

The people of Athens watched the ships slicing through the waves as they approached. Every man, woman and child looked on in fear. As soon as the ships reached the quayside, King Minos and his soldiers leapt ashore. They marched through the streets of Athens and wherever they saw a young man of noble bearing King Minos would shout, "Seize him!"

Six young men had been taken by the time they had reached the palace of King Aegeus. Standing behind the king's throne was a youth with a crown of laurel leaves on his head. He looked like a god. He could almost have been Ares, the beautiful god of war. Minos shouted: "He will be the seventh!"

King Aegeus fell to the ground at Minos's feet. "Please!" he cried. "He is my own son, my only son, Theseus. I beg you, spare his life."

Minos kicked Aegeus aside. "Seize the prince!" he commanded.

But before the soldiers could grab him, Theseus stepped forward. "No need to bind my arms," he said. "I come happily, of my own free will. I look forward to meeting your Minotaur."

The seven Athenian youths boarded an Athenian ship. It was a ship with black sails, because everyone believed that they were sailing to their deaths.

The next morning King Aegeus went down to the quayside, accompanied by a beautiful young Athenian woman called Aegle. Aegle saw Theseus leaning over the rail of the ship. She threw her arms around his neck. "Theseus, you will not forget me, will you?" she cried.

"Aegle, I will never forget you, and when I return I will make you a queen of Athens."

Then King Aegeus spoke to his son, "Theseus, if you die it will break my heart. But if, by the grace of the mighty gods, you return safely home to Athens, please, I beg you, swap these black sails for white ones, so that I may know the best or the worst before any word reaches me."

Theseus bowed his head. "Father, I promise. I will do so," he said.

Then the ropes were untied and the black-sailed ship left the quayside, surrounded by the white-sailed ships of King Minos.

CHAPTER SIX

LOVE IN A DANGEROUS TIME

OR THREE DAYS AND THREE nights they sailed. When they reached the island of Crete there was a blaring of horns and trumpets to greet the king on his return. The seven Athenian youths were led to the palace in a glittering procession. They were invited to sit down to a feast. But as they tasted the delicious meats and sipped the sweet wines, they could hear the sound of keys turning in locks. They knew that they were trapped.

They slept that night between silken sheets and beneath purple blankets. But the next morning there were only six of them at the breakfast table. As they ate they heard the distant sound of screaming from somewhere far below. Five pushed their plates away, but Theseus chewed his food and listened.

King Minos entertained his guests. They were invited to compete with the finest Cretan runners, leapers, wrestlers and archers. Theseus defeated them all. In the evenings, Princess Ariadne would dance for them, her blazing crown upon her head, making the shadows of the great hall leap around her.

So the days went by. Then, one morning, there were five of them at the breakfast table. Then there were four.

Ariadne could not take her eyes off Theseus. When he was running or wrestling,

she would be watching him. When she was dancing, her eyes were fixed on him. Theseus felt the weight of her gaze and smiled to himself.

Then there were three of them at the breakfast table. Then two.

When no one was watching, Theseus seized Ariadne by the hand. "Ariadne, from the moment I first saw you I have loved you. I could have made you so happy. I could have taken you to Athens. I could have made you a queen."

She looked at him and tears spilled down her cheeks. Then, shaking her head, she pulled her hand away and ran from the room.

One morning, Theseus found that he was alone at the breakfast table. He waited for his chance and then approached the princess again.

"Ariadne, is there nobody who can help me?" he said. "If I could escape, I would take you with me."

Ariadne could not help herself. She melted into his arms, pressing her lips to his. "Yes, yes, there is someone..." Then, breaking from his embrace, she ran to find Daedalus.

CHAPTER SEVEN

A CUNNING PLAN

"**I** WANT YOU TO HELP THIS Theseus defeat my brother," Ariadne said to Daedalus.

Daedalus shook his head. "I cannot," he replied. "Your father would be furious with me."

"You must. If you don't, I will tell my father about your secret son. Oh yes, I have seen what my parents have not. I have seen young Icarus. And when my father lays eyes on your boy, you know as well as I what will happen. Icarus will be sent into the maze to be devoured. So you have no choice but to help Theseus!"

Daedalus bowed his head and set to work. That night he slipped out of the palace and placed inside the entrance to the maze the things Theseus would need to defeat the monster.

Meanwhile, Ariadne crept into Theseus's gilded bedchamber. Leaning over the bed, she whispered, "My love, when they take you to the labyrinth, feel among the shadows to your left. You will find my crown to light your way. You will find a ball of golden thread so that you won't get lost. And you will find a bronze sword . . . for my brother. When you have finished, wait by the entrance of the labyrinth until nightfall and I will meet you outside." She kissed him and slipped away.

The next morning, King Minos was amazed. Theseus emerged from his bedchamber

of his own free will. There was no need to drag him from his room screaming and shouting. Surely by now he understood his fate? Why was he so relaxed — chatting to the guards and cracking jokes?

Down to the maze they went. Theseus was shown to the entrance of the labyrinth. He stepped inside. The darkness swallowed him, and there was silence.

CHAPTER EIGHT

INTO THE LABYRINTH

J UST AS ARIADNE HAD TOLD HIM,
Theseus felt among the shadows to his left.
His fingers closed around her crown and he
lifted it onto his head. He felt for the two stones
and struck them together. The crown blazed
with light. He found the ball of golden thread
and tied the end to a snag of rock. Picking up
the bronze sword, he began to make his way
into the labyrinth. He followed the tunnels
as they forked right and left, unwinding the
thread as he went. Above his head the shadows

danced. Beneath his feet were shreds of rag and splinters of bone picked clean.

Suddenly, he could hear the creature, grunting and snorting. Then he could smell it: the sour smell of sweat mingling with the sickly sweet stench of rotten flesh. Then he saw it: the human body, the great bull's head — the Minotaur.

Asterius had never seen such brightness before. Ariadne's crown blazed with light, and he was filled with terror. He lurched and lost his balance, blinded.

Theseus laughed. This was easy! He plunged his sword into the beast's belly.

Asterius, still reeling in the bright light, felt something pierce his skin. He screamed...

Up above, Minos heard the screaming. That was a human sound. A human was dying, not a monster. Theseus was dead!

Again and again, Theseus stabbed the Minotaur. He stabbed its neck, its arms, its thighs, its chest. He opened up a constellation of wounds. The beast sank to its knees. Theseus seized it by one of its horns and hacked off its head.

Dragging the head in one hand and winding in the golden thread with the other, he made his way back through the tunnels as they twisted to the right and to the left. At last he saw the entrance to the labyrinth. He crouched down and waited until nightfall.

When the stars began to shine in the sky above, Theseus emerged from the labyrinth. Ariadne was waiting for him. He lifted the great bull's head, the head of her brother, and thrust it onto a stake at the entrance to the maze. Then he seized Ariadne by the hand and they ran to the quayside, where the Athenian ship was still moored. They jumped onto the deck of the ship and Theseus ordered the crew to cut the ropes. Before they departed they set fire to all the Cretan ships, so that a black pall of smoke rose into the sky, extinguishing the light of the stars. Then they sailed away.

CHAPTER NINE

DAEDALUS PAYS THE PRICE

"**Y**OUR HIGHNESSES MUST come at once!" a servant cried.

King Minos and Queen Pasiphae looked out and saw smoke rising from the quayside. They went to their daughter's bedchamber... her bed was empty! They rushed to the maze to find the dripping head of Asterius on a stake. Minos ground his teeth. Pasiphae cradled the head of her son and wept bitter tears.

Soldiers were sent to the chambers of Daedalus. They found him with a young man. They were so alike that the boy had to be Daedalus's son. Both of them were dragged before the king.

"Look where all your cleverness has brought us!" cried Minos. "My fleet is at the bottom of the sea, and my daughter has fled with that Athenian trickster Theseus! You will pay for this."

"Your highness, I beg you," pleaded Daedalus. "Please don't put us into that dark place below!"

The king grinned. "You will rot in this maze of your own making," he replied.

Daedalus and Icarus were slung into the labyrinth. Daedalus reached up to a secret ledge. He had hidden an oil lamp and some other supplies there. He lit the lamp and set to work.

A pigeon was nesting in a crevice. He caught it and stretched out its left wing. Taking the furthermost feather between finger and thumb, he pulled. The bird shrieked and flew up. Daedalus snatched it from the air. He stretched out the right wing. He took the furthermost feather between finger and thumb and pulled. Each time he removed a feather he studied the bird's attempts at flight . . . and he learned much.

Icarus watched, fascinated. He saw a fluffy feather at his feet. He picked it up and blew. It lifted at the command of his breath . . . then fell.

CHAPTER TEN

LOVE BETRAYED

RIADNE AND THESEUS
sailed towards Athens. Ariadne had
never been so happy. There was a fair wind, and
after two days they came to the island of Naxos.
Theseus suggested they go ashore for fresh meat
and fruit. That night they lit a fire on the beach.
They ate, they talked, they laughed, they danced.
Then they slept in the warmth of the fire.

In the middle of the night, Ariadne woke.
She was alone. She sat up and looked about.
By the light of the moon she could see the

Athenian ship. She could see the anchor being lifted and the sails being unfurled. She ran down to the water's edge. "Theseus!" she cried.

From the deck of the ship came the sound of mocking laughter. There was a thud at her feet, then another, then a third. Looking down, she saw her crown, the ball of golden thread and the bronze sword lying on the sand. The wind filled the sails, the prow of the ship sliced through the waves, and Theseus was gone. He had vanished into the night.

Ariadne dropped to her knees, buried her face in her hands and trembled with sobs.

But nothing is hidden from the mighty gods. Dionysus, the god of drinking and drunkenness, of madness and ecstasy, of wild dancing and wild music, saw her and felt pity stirring in his heart. He came down from the heavens and lifted her to her feet.

"Ariadne," he said, "Theseus might have broken his promise to make you a queen of Athens...but I will make a promise that I will keep. I will make you a queen of the heavens."

He took her crown and set it in the sky as the constellation Corona Borealis. Then he led her up to the high slopes of Mount Olympus where she became his consort, his queen.

Theseus sailed homewards. All day he sailed. And as the sun was sinking, he saw the city of Athens ahead of him. He saw people standing on the cliff tops looking out to sea. He scanned the cliffs, sheltering his eyes from the sun. Was Aegle there waiting for him, and perhaps his father too?

Then suddenly he saw a figure falling, flailing, plunging from cliff to sea. Who could it be? He looked up and his heart sank. He had forgotten to swap the black sails for white ones.

His father, King Aegeus, thinking his son was dead, had hurled himself to his death.

Soon Theseus could see his father's broken body bobbing in the waves. With a boat hook, he lifted him onto the deck of the ship. He knelt beside the dripping corpse of Aegeus. And for the first time in his life, Theseus knew sorrow.

And ever since then, that body of water has been known as the Aegean Sea.

CHAPTER ELEVEN

ICARUS FLIES

IN CRETE, DAEDALUS HAD ONCE again bent nature to his will. With the bones of the dead, beeswax, feathers and linen thread, he had made two pairs of wonderful wings, one pair for himself and one for Icarus.

One night, just before dawn, Daedalus woke Icarus and whispered urgently to him. "Listen to me, my son," he said. "Minos controls both land and sea, but he cannot control the air. You and I will fly to freedom. It is still dark, but follow me. When day breaks, you must remember this: if you fly too high, the heat of the sun will melt the wax that binds feather to bone. If you fly too low, the waves will splash against your wings and their sodden weight will drag you down. Follow me and ride the gusts I ride."

They went outside. The sky was filled with stars. No soldiers guarded the entrance to the labyrinth. There was no need — Minos controlled both land and sea. Under cover of darkness, Daedalus and Icarus made their way to the top of a cliff. They strapped on the wings. They embraced. Then they ran to the cliff edge and leapt, beating their feathered arms against the air...

They rose! They rose into the cool night sky! Every surging gust of wind made Icarus cry out with joy. All his life he had hidden in dusty corners for fear of King Minos. Now the sweep of the broad sky was above him, and the dark sea beneath! He saw a band of red ahead. Day was coming. Island after island passed by beneath, some no more than barren rocks jutting out of the sea, some much bigger and dotted with farms and villages. Icarus laughed at the little figures as they shouted and pointed far below. Higher he flew, and higher again.

A gust of wind lifted him. He lurched. A feather fell. He looked up to see the bird that had shed it, but his gaze met only the fierce eye of the hot sun. A shower of feathers was fluttering down now ...

Daedalus turned to look back. Icarus was no longer following him, but tumbling, flailing, screaming as he plunged headlong into the sea.

In desperation, Daedalus flew to the nearest island and found a fishing boat. He

rowed out across the water and retrieved the corpse of his son.

His hot tears splashed against the boy's face, and for the first time, Daedalus knew sorrow.

And ever since then, that body of water has been known as the Icarian Sea.

In the burial grounds of the city of Athens, a son said farewell to his father. As Theseus walked away from the grave of old Aegeus, he was aware of a strange light blazing high overhead. He looked up. There was a new constellation in the sky, a circlet of mocking stars — Ariadne's shining crown.

Meanwhile, on a small island, a father buried his son. As Daedalus dug the grave, he too glimpsed something in the sky. He looked up to see a black and white bird rising and plunging. Every time the bird plummeted,

Daedalus thought of his son and sobbed.
Then he remembered another falling boy. He
remembered Talos, whom he had pushed from
a cliff in Athens.

Daedalus watched the lapwing mocking
him, and he wept.

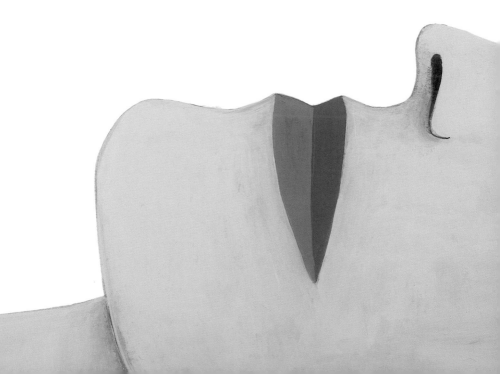

MORE ABOUT THE MYTH

The story of Theseus and the Minotaur is found in two important places: a poem by the Roman writer Ovid, and an essay by the Greek author Plutarch. Ancient sources don't always tell myths the same way — Plutarch's version of the story does not include Icarus and his flight too close to the sun, but Ovid's does.

Many works of art have taken inspiration from this myth, from Dante's *Inferno* (written in the 14th century) to Chaucer's *The Canterbury Tales* (written 1387–1400) to Shakespeare's *A Midsummer Night's Dream* (written 1595–1596). Author Suzanne Collins says she was inspired to write the Hunger Games trilogy (published 2008–2010) by the myth of Theseus and the Minotaur.

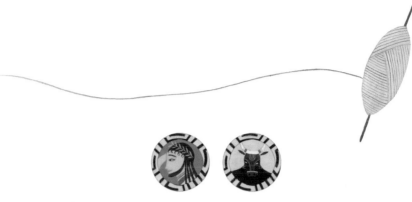

THESEUS was an important hero for the ancient Greeks, who considered him responsible for uniting the region of Attica under the rule of the city of Athens. Theseus appears in several famous Greek myths. He is known for the story of the six challenges he overcame on his journey to Athens. He also sailed with Jason in the myth of Jason and the Argonauts, and he appears in the myth of Phaedra and Hippolytus as well.

The **MINOTAUR**'s name means "the bull of Minos," after King Minos. This creature, with the head of a bull and the body of a man, does not appear in other Greek myths.

Characters in the Story

Orpheus & Eurydice

(OR-fee-us)   *(yur-RID-uh-see)*
a musician   Orpheus's wife

Hades & Persephone

(HAY-deez)   *(per-SEH-fon-ee)*
god of the   Hades's wife and
Underworld   Demeter's daughter

Charon

(CARE-on)
Underworld ferryman

Cerberus

(KER-ber-us)
Underworld guard dog

The Three Fates

goddesses of destiny

Dionysus

(DIE-oh-nice-us)
god of wine

The Angry Women

Apollo

(uh-PAUL-oh)
god of the sun

ORPHEUS
········· AND ·········
EURYDICE

A WEDDING AND
A FUNERAL

T HERE HAS ONLY BEEN ONE
mortal man whose skill at playing the
lyre compared with that of the god of music,
golden Apollo.

His name was Orpheus. When he played,
the birds would swoop down from the heavens
and perch on the branches above his head.
When he played, the animals of the fields
would gather around him, their heads cocked
to one side as they listened to him. It was said

that when he played even the trees would dance. Have you ever seen trees standing in circles and avenues? It is said that those are the places where Orpheus stopped playing before the dance was finished. In those places we can still see the patterns of the dance.

Now, Orpheus had fallen in love with a woman called Eurydice. There was a wedding, a magnificent wedding with many guests and delicious food to eat. All the master musicians were there, playing instruments of every kind.

But all through the wedding ceremony the candles and lamps in the temple gave off an oily black smoke, so that the guests coughed and choked. Even the priests had to wipe tears from their eyes. They looked at one another and shook their heads. "This is a bad omen," they said. "Such things should never happen at a wedding."

The priests had good reason to be worried.

The morning after the wedding, Eurydice
woke up early. She climbed out of bed while
Orpheus was still deep in sleep. She pulled on
her clothes and slipped outside.

Dawn was breaking. The warm autumn light woke a snake that was coiled up on a rock. It slid through the grass just as Eurydice was stepping barefoot across the meadow. Their paths crossed. Startled, the snake sank its fangs into Eurydice's ankle. Its poison coursed through her veins. With a cry she fell to the ground.

When Orpheus found her, she was lying dead and cold in the dew-damp grass. He lifted her in his arms. He carried her home, his face wet with tears.

And so it came about that the day after their wedding was the day of Eurydice's funeral. The wedding guests, who the day before had gathered in joy, now gathered in sorrow as her body was laid on a pyre, piled high with wood.

Coins were placed over her eyes to pay the ferryman who would carry her across the water to the Land of the Dead. Blazing torches were lowered into the kindling, and as the flames wrapped themselves around his wife's body, Orpheus stood and watched, bowed down with a terrible sorrow.

THE JOURNEY BEGINS

WHEN THE FUNERAL WAS over, when the heat of the fire had turned Eurydice's bones to fine white ash, Orpheus picked up his lyre and set off on a great adventure.

He journeyed for many days over land and sea until he came to a dark cave. He entered the cave and followed it down and down, making his way through tunnels that twisted to the left and right. Orpheus continued deeper and deeper into darkness. He waded across a river of blood. He waded across a river of tears. He passed through an orchard, its fruit sweet with the stench of decay. He passed through a forest of swords and knives.

He came at last to the edge of a dark, oily river: the River of Forgetfulness. It is the river that separates the living from the dead. Once a dead person's soul has crossed over it, they lose all memory of how they have lived and of those they have loved. On the far side, Orpheus could make out the shadowy hills of the country he was seeking: the Land of the Dead.

He stared across the water with only the thought of Eurydice in his mind. How could his lovely bride be there, in that strange dark place? He lifted his lyre to his shoulder and began to play a tune that brimmed with love and sorrow.

The beauty of the music floated out across the deep, dark water. It reached the ears of the

ferryman, Charon. He poled his boat in the
direction of the sound.

When he saw Orpheus he said, "Stranger,
whether you are mortal or immortal, living or

dead, your music so enchants my ears that I will carry you across the water free of charge. Climb into my boat."

Orpheus stepped from the bank into the boat, and the ancient ferryman pushed away from the land and poled across the river. When they reached the far side, Orpheus lowered his lyre, jumped ashore and strode into the dark shadows.

Suddenly there came the sound of growling, then a harsh barking. Out of the shadows leapt Cerberus, the great three-headed dog who guards the riverbank. He rushed at Orpheus, his hackles up, his lips curled back to show huge yellow teeth.

Lifting his lyre, Orpheus began to play again. Such was the beauty of his music that Cerberus stopped in his tracks. The monstrous dog wagged his tail and closed his six red eyes.

He rolled onto his back and howled with all three of his mouths.

Soon there was a whispering around Orpheus, a rustling, a shuffling, like the sound of the wind blowing through dried leaves. The dead were gathering. They were following him. They were enchanted by his music. It made them weep for sorrows they could not remember anymore; it made them laugh for joys that were forgotten. For the dead have lost all memory of their lives; they are a drifting host of whispering ghosts.

THE SORROW OF HADES

O N A N D O N O R P H E U S walked, surrounded by the spirits of the dead. Then a palace loomed out of the shadows, a great palace with towering black walls. As he approached it, the dead fell back. He found that he was walking alone. He was approaching the dwelling place of their king. He made his way between black gates. He climbed steps of black stone. Doors of black ebony swung open before him and he stepped into a vast and gloomy hall.

At the far end of it, there were two thrones. On one sat the king of terrors, Hades, his eyes as deep as open graves, his thick beard spread across his chest. Beside Hades sat his wife, beautiful Persephone. She was like the moon shining in a dark sky, like a pale mistletoe berry in the depths of winter. It was early autumn, and she had returned to her grim husband for the chill months of winter, after bringing spring and summer to the Land of the Living.

Orpheus, still playing his lyre, walked up to the two thrones. He stood before the god and goddess. He looked into their faces. And then he began to sing,

> "We mortals are wretched things,
> and the gods who know no care
> have woven sorrow
> into the pattern of our lives.
> Even the sparrow on the branch,
> even the wren in the willow
> knows more of sorrow
> than the thundering gods,
> who have never felt the cold, cold hand
> of death about their hearts.

"But you mighty gods,

though you have never known death,

you have suffered the sweet pains of love.

You have felt the piercing shafts

from Aphrodite's shining bow.

Great Hades,

imagine those long months

when Persephone returns

to the bright world above

lasting forever.

Imagine, if you can,

her pale face crumbling into dust.

That is how it is for mortal man.

Great Hades, give me back my Eurydice.

I beg you, give her back to me."

There was a silence. Then Persephone turned to Hades, her face streaming with silver tears. And Hades turned to his wife. One oily black tear trickled down his cheek and splashed onto his beard. He drew breath and said, "Fetch me the three Fates."

The three ancient sisters were brought before him. The three Fates who control the destinies of men and women: one spins out the thread of a life; the second measures its length; and the third cuts it. Hades looked into the wrinkled, leathery face of the third sister. "Find the cut thread of Eurydice's life . . . and mend it!"

The third sister bowed before the god and swiftly departed.

Hades turned to Orpheus. "Now go!" he said. "Leave my palace. Leave my kingdom . . . and Eurydice will follow you. But never once look behind you. Do not look over your shoulder until the light of the sun shines full upon your face."

THE JOURNEY HOME

O RPHEUS BOWED, TURNED on his heel and left the palace. He made his way across the shadowy kingdom until he came to the river's edge.

Charon the ferryman was waiting for him. Orpheus climbed into the boat. As he sat down, he felt it tremble as though someone had climbed in behind him. He kept his eyes fixed on the shore.

When they reached the riverbank, he stepped out of the boat. Behind him he could hear footsteps, soft footsteps following him.

He journeyed through the forest; he journeyed through the orchard; he crossed the two rivers. Sometimes he could hear the snap of a twig behind him, sometimes the splashing of feet other than his own. Sometimes he thought he could feel a gentle breath on the back of his neck. Still he looked ahead.

He came to the tunnel of stone, winding to left and right. And then, at last, Orpheus was out of the cave, breathing the fresh air of the living world once again. Above him, the sky was bright with shining stars. "Soon," he thought to himself, "soon the dawn will break and the light of the sun will shine on my face."

But just behind him, Eurydice suddenly caught her foot on a stone. She tripped and she fell. Orpheus heard her stumble and, without thinking, he turned to catch her in his arms. He tried to break her fall . . . and for a single moment he saw her face, pale beneath the silver stars. Then his arms closed around empty air and she was gone.

The third Fate had cut the thread of Eurydice's life for the second time ... and this time there would be no mending it.

Orpheus turned. He ran back into the cave, he journeyed down into darkness, he crossed the rivers, the orchard and the forest. He did not stop until he had reached the River of Forgetfulness. Standing on the riverbank, he shouted her name across the dark, oily water. But there was no answer.

Three-headed Cerberus rushed out from the shadows, growling and snarling. Charon the ancient ferryman cursed him and spat at him, refusing to carry him across. Orpheus knew he could go no further. He could not return to Hades.

So he made his way back to the living

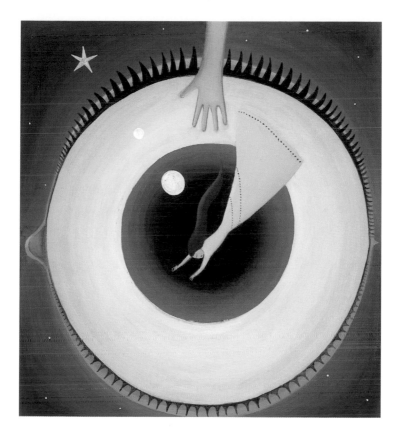

world and he devoted himself to his music,
which was more beautiful than ever, woven
through with a silver thread of sorrow. It was all
he was interested in now, all he could care for.
He devoted himself to the worship of golden

Apollo, the god of music. And he devoted himself to the memory of his beloved Eurydice.

His music was so beautiful that many women fell in love with him, but Orpheus did not care. He did not even notice their attentions. He stayed true to the memory of Eurydice and turned his back on them all.

A GOD'S FURY

BUT THE BEAUTY OF HIS MUSIC also drifted up into the heavens. It reached the ears of one of the gods, Dionysus, the god of drinking and drunkenness, of madness and ecstasy, of wild dancing and wild music. He was filled with jealous rage. He cried out, "Why does Orpheus devote all his music to golden Apollo, and none of it to me?"

Dionysus looked down at the world and saw all the women whom Orpheus had turned his back on. Dionysus frowned . . . and with his frown those women were filled with his own jealous fury. They were maddened with a god's raging envy.

The women couldn't help themselves. They ran to the place where Orpheus was playing his lyre with the birds and animals gathered around him. They picked up stones and clods of earth and threw them at him.

But the music was so beautiful that the stones did not touch Orpheus. They dropped to the ground at his feet. So the women began to scream. The sound of their screams drowned the music, and the stones and clods began to strike Orpheus. The birds rose up into the sky. The animals fled.

Orpheus pleaded with the women to leave him alone. But they ran into a field. They found spades and sickles and the blade of a shovel. They attacked Orpheus. They hacked off his

head. They lifted it up and flung it into a river.
They picked up his lyre and flung it in behind.

The head and the lyre drifted downstream,
bobbing in the water like apples. Then a strange
thing happened. The head of Orpheus opened

its mouth and began to sing. The lyre began to play of its own accord. Together they made a music so beautiful that the whole world held its breath. The trees bowed their branches and shed their leaves.

EVER AFTER

THE HEAD AND THE LYRE were carried by the river to the sea, singing and playing. Then they were carried by the tides and the currents and the waves of the sea. They were carried to the island of Lesbos. They were washed up on the seashore, still singing and playing.

The people of Lesbos found the miraculous head. They carried it to a cave and sat and listened to it, enchanted by the beauty of its music.

Golden Apollo reached down from the heavens and lifted up the lyre. He set it in the night sky as a constellation — a pattern of stars called The Lyre that we can still see to this day.

And as for Orpheus, he journeyed for the third time down to the River of Forgetfulness. He was a spirit himself now and Charon the ferryman was waiting for him. He was carried across the water. As he stepped onto the bank at the far side, like all the others, he forgot everything. Orpheus joined the drifting hosts of the dead.

But Persephone, the wife of Hades, saw him and remembered him. She felt pity stirring in her heart. She reached out and touched his forehead with the tip of her finger.

In that moment Orpheus's memory returned. She touched Eurydice's forehead and she, too, remembered everything. The

two lovers found one another in that shadowy kingdom and they fell into each other's arms.

And even to this day they walk together, talking, singing and laughing. Sometimes they walk arm in arm. Sometimes Eurydice walks ahead and Orpheus follows. Sometimes

Orpheus walks ahead, knowing that he can look over his shoulder, and his Eurydice will always be there.

MORE ABOUT THE MYTH

We know Orpheus and Eurydice's story from two poems written in Latin — one by a poet named Ovid and the other by a poet named Virgil. Stories similar to Orpheus and Eurydice's can be found in Japanese, Mayan, Indian and even biblical literature.

This love story has inspired countless retellings by artists of all kinds, from ancient Roman senator Boethius to modern-day American musical group She & Him. Italian painter Titian and French sculptor Rodin both created pieces called "Orpheus and Eurydice" — Titian around 1511 and Rodin in 1893. The story has also been told in poems, films, plays, songs, operas, comics and even video games.

ORPHEUS is the son of Apollo, the god of the sun, and Calliope, the Muse of epic poetry. He was revered by Greeks as the greatest musician of all time, and was even worshipped in a religion called Orphism. He also appears in the myth of Jason and the Argonauts. In that story, Jason brings Orpheus along on his quest for the golden fleece to help him get past the dangerous Sirens, whose enchanting singing lures sailors to wreck their ships. Orpheus saves the day by drowning out the singing of the Sirens with his lyre.

EURYDICE, on the other hand, is not mentioned in ancient sources outside of this myth. Her name means "she whose justice extends widely."

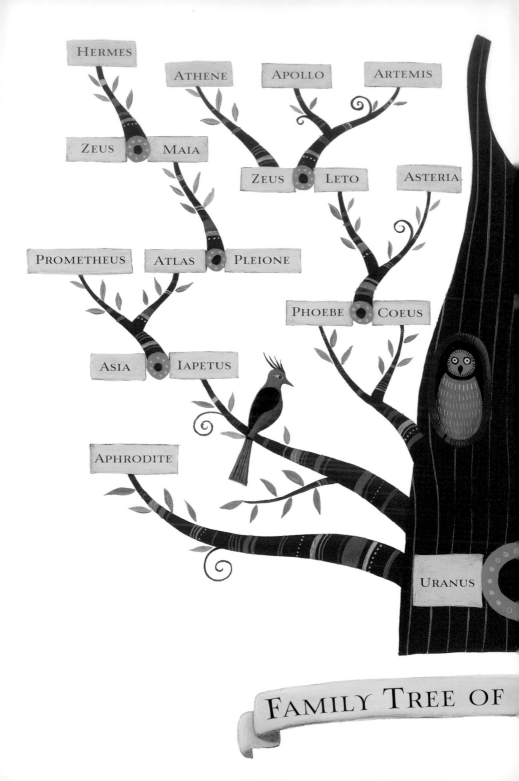

HERMES

ATHENE   APOLLO   ARTEMIS

ZEUS   MAIA

ZEUS   LETO   ASTERIA

PROMETHEUS   ATLAS   PLEIONE

PHOEBE   COEUS

ASIA   IAPETUS

APHRODITE

URANUS

FAMILY TREE OF

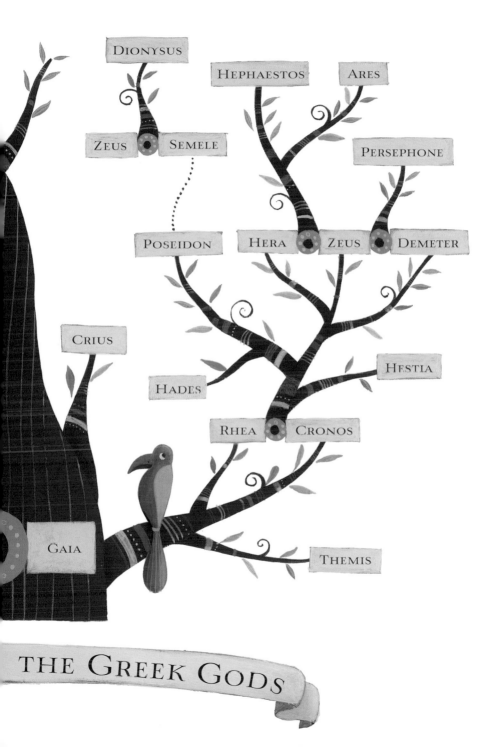

THE GREEK GODS

ZEUS
GOD OF THUNDER

HERA
GODDESS OF MARRIAGE

APHRODITE
GODDESS OF LOVE

POSEIDON
GOD OF THE SEA

APOLLO
GOD OF THE SUN

ATHENE
GODDESS OF WISDOM

Olympians

DIONYSUS
GOD OF WINE

ARTEMIS
GODDESS OF THE HUNT

DEMETER
GODDESS OF THE HARVEST

ARES
GOD OF WAR

HEPHAESTOS
GOD OF FIRE

HERMES
MESSENGER GOD

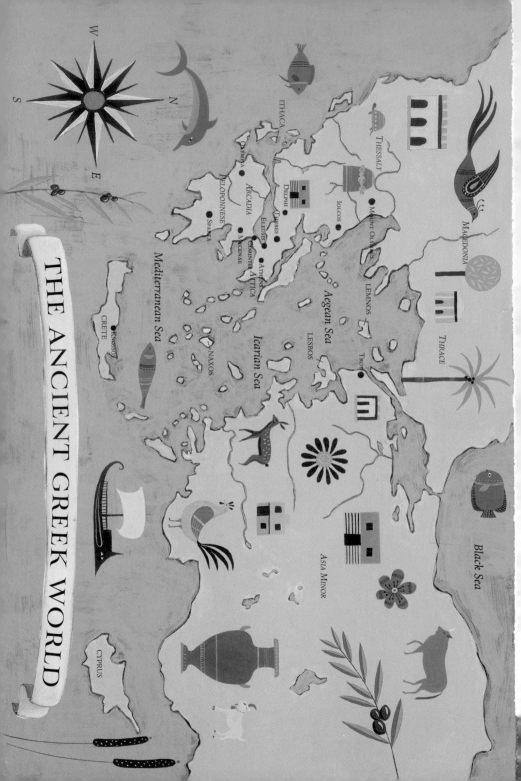

THE ANCIENT GREEK WORLD

W
N
S
E

Mediterranean Sea

ITHACA
OLYMPIA
PELOPONNESE
ARCADIA
SPARTA
DELPHI
ELEUSIS
THEBES
CORINTH
MYCENAE
ATHENS
ATTICA

THESSALY
IOLCOS
Mount Olympus
MACEDONIA
THRACE

CRETE
KNOSSOS

NAXOS

Icarian Sea

Aegean Sea

LEMNOS
LESBOS
TROY

ASIA MINOR

Black Sea

CYPRUS